Blue's Clues®

A Visit to the Firehouse

by Lauryn Silverhardt
illustrated by Karen Craig

Simon Spotlight/Nickelodeon
New York   London   Toronto   Sydney

Based on the TV series *Blue's Clues*® created by Traci Paige Johnson,
Todd Kessler, and Angela C. Santomero as seen on Nick Jr.®

SIMON SPOTLIGHT
An imprint of Simon & Schuster Children's Publishing Division
1230 Avenue of the Americas, New York, New York 10020
© 2009 Viacom International Inc. All rights reserved. NICK JR., *Blue's Clues, Blue's Room,*
and all related titles, logos, and characters are trademarks of Viacom International Inc.
Created by Traci Paige Johnson, Todd Kessler, and Angela C. Santomero.
All rights reserved, including the right of reproduction in whole or in part in any form.
SIMON SPOTLIGHT and colophon are registered trademarks of Simon & Schuster, Inc.
Manufactured in the United States of America
10 9 8 7 6 5 4 3
ISBN: 978-1-4169-7193-1

Blue, Sprinkles, Frederica, and Roar E. Saurus were having a make-believe town playdate.

"Rarrrrrrr . . . rarrrrrrr! Coming through!" shouted Sprinkles, imitating the sound of a siren as he pushed along his shiny red fire truck.

"I'm Officer Frederica, and I am here to help!"
exclaimed Frederica as she picked up her toy police car.
"It's my job to help people and make sure they are safe!"
Blue was pretending to be a construction worker.
"Watch out below!" bellowed Blue
as she moved her crane.

"Toot! Toot! All aboard!" announced Conductor Roar E. Saurus. "I can take you to lots of different places. Next train is leaving in one minute."

"What are you building, Builder Blue?" asked Sprinkles.
"I'm building . . . a playground!" Blue answered.

"Neat!" cried Officer Frederica. "Just what this town needs—a really good playground for kids to play in!"

"When it's all finished, I will take my passengers to visit your playground," added Conductor Roar E. Saurus.

Sprinkles looked a little discouraged.

"What's wrong, little brother?" asked Blue.

"Everyone else knows what job they have to do, but I really don't know how to be a fireman," answered Sprinkles.

"Hmm," said Blue. "I have an idea. Why don't we go visit a real fire station and see what firefighters do?"

"Good thinking!" exclaimed Frederica.

"Do you think we'll get to climb on a *real* fire truck?" asked Sprinkles.

"Let's find out!" answered Blue with excitement. "We'll get there by jumping into this picture. Ready, everyone?"

"Ready!" exclaimed Frederica.

"Ready-asaurus!" roared Roar E. Saurus.

"Let's go!"
cried Sprinkles.

"Hi, all!" said the fireman. "My name is Fireman Dave. Welcome to the town fire station."

"Hi, Fireman Dave," Blue said. "I'm Blue, and this is my little brother, Sprinkles. We want to learn all about firefighters!"

"Why don't you come on into the station, and I can tell you all about it," replied Fireman Dave, waving for them to follow him inside.

"So Fireman Dave, what does a fireman do?" asked Blue.

"Well, if there is a fire, we make sure people safely get out of the building, and then we set up our hoses and put the fire out!" he answered.

DIAL 911

Then Fireman Dave added, "We also rescue animals that get stuck
n trees."

"Wow!" Sprinkles smiled.

"Would you like a tour of the fire station?" asked Fireman Dave.

"Yes, please!" they responded in unison.

"See this phone?" asked Fireman Dave. "Well, whenever there is someone in town who needs our help, we receive a call on *this* phone."

"Wow, kind of like how superheroes get calls for help," exclaimed Sprinkles.

"Firefighters are real-world superheroes," Blue replied.

Then Fireman Dave pointed out their uniforms.

"We keep our uniforms out here so we can get dressed and out of he station superfast!" said the fireman.

"Once we are all dressed and ready to go, we slide down this pole, climb aboard the fire truck, and off we go!" said Fireman Dave as he slid down the pole.

Fireman Dave landed safely on the ground, and then he invited Blue, Sprinkles, and their friends to slide down the pole too.

"I really want to," said Sprinkles, "but . . . I'm a little scared."

"Not to worry," replied Fireman Dave. "I will make sure you land smooth and safely—after all, it's my job!"

Sprinkles smiled and hopped onto the pole. And down the pole he went.

Blue, Frederica, and Roar E. Saurus quickly followed.

"Wheeeee!" exclaimed Blue.

"That was great!" cried Frederica.

"Here I come!" roared Roar E. Saurus.

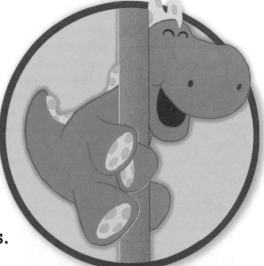

Once they all landed, Fireman
Dave invited them to climb aboard
the fire truck.

"Really?" asked Sprinkles in disbelief.

"Absolutely!"

"Sprinkles, you look like you are ready to go rescue some people," said Frederica.

"And don't forget cats in trees too!" Sprinkles said with a laugh.

"But you are missing one thing," Fireman Dave said, putting his firefighter hat on Sprinkles' head. "There! Now you are ready to be a fireman!"

"Thanks, Fireman Dave!" cried Sprinkles.

"What a great day!" exclaimed Blue.

"Definitely!" roared Roar E. Saurus.

"You know something, Sprinkles," said Frederica. "That hat goes nicely with your shiny red fire truck."

"Thanks, Fred," said Sprinkles, adjusting his new hat. "Now let's go help some people out in our town!"